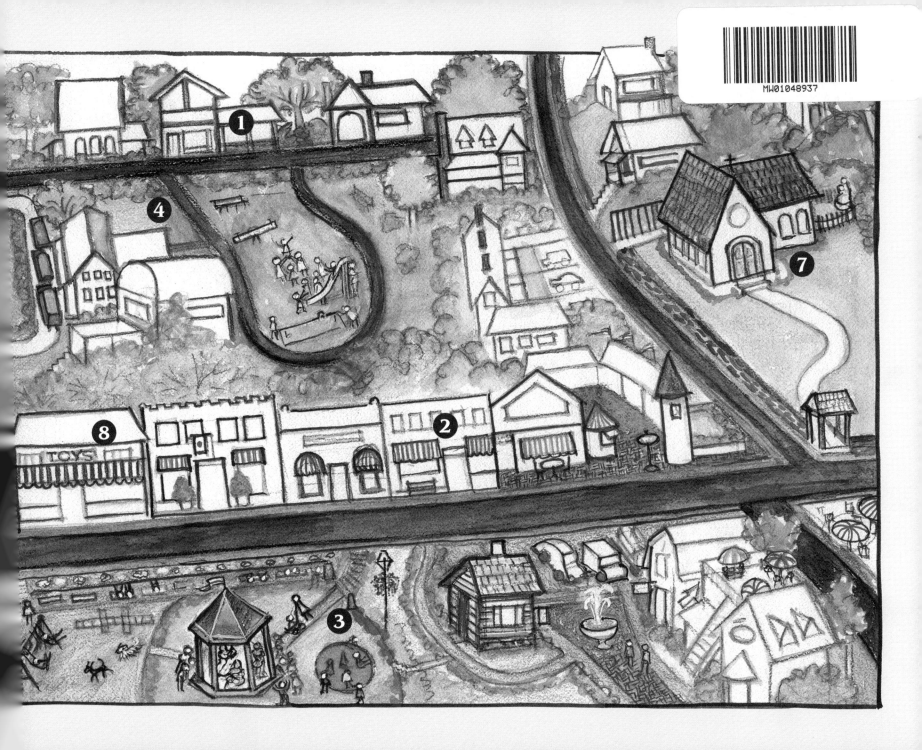

Isabella Propeller
and the Magic Beanie

by Jonathan Graves
Illustrated by Gail Haley

To my grandchildren: Isabelle, Evy, Gray, Stanton and Martha Grace.
And to my wife and best friend, Lucy.

There are certain places in the world
where stories never grow old.
They become new again with each generation of listeners.

This story happened in just such a place,
in a village on top of a high mountain.

It's a place with strange—and some say—magical winds...
a place called Blowing Rock.

It was a gray, blustery Saturday, just the kind of day Isabella loved. As the winds whistled around the little cottage, Isabella was snug in her grandparents' attic, playing dress-up with her dog, Mullaby.

Suddenly, the attic window blew open with a bang, and cool winds began swirling around the room, scattering papers and attic treasures everywhere.

Isabella rushed to latch the window. "Uh-oh," she said, looking at the big mess the winds had made. "Grandma LuLu won't be happy about this."

Mullaby gave a muffled bark.

"What've you got there, girl?" Isabella asked.
She reached down and took something colorful from the dog's mouth.

It was a funny little hat with a propeller on the top! Isabella plopped it on her head. Right away, she felt a warm, tingly sensation—all the way down to her toes.

Maybe it's magic, she thought.

But where did it come from?

Isabella bounded down the
stairs to the kitchen. "Pop!
LuLu! Look what I found!"
she called. "May I keep it?"

"That old beanie? Sure,"
LuLu replied, sipping her tea.
"But where did you get it?"

"Up in the attic. Mullaby
found it."

"Well, it certainly looks good on you," Pop said, giving the beanie's propeller a playful spin. "I guess from now on, we'll have to call you Isabella Propeller!"

Just then, Isabella's brother Trip and her cousin Ginny burst through the door.

"The wind's stopped!" Trip shouted. "Now we can have the picnic you promised us, LuLu!"

"Let's go to the Blowing Rock," Ginny suggested. "I wanna see the place where the Indian brave fell over the cliff and got blown back up by the winds."

Trip scoffed. "You don't believe that old mountain story, do you? No wind is that strong."

"*I believe it,*" Isabella said. "Winds can do anything."

Trip rolled his eyes. Then he saw Isabella's beanie. "Hey, where'd you get that stupid hat?"

"None of your business," Isabella quipped.

While Trip and Ginny helped make sandwiches, Isabella and Pop took the dog for a walk. "Wait here a minute," Pop said, as they passed Willard's Ice Cream Shop. "I'll be right back."

Isabella plopped down on a bench next to an old woman. She was wearing a swirly, colorful shawl. "It's nice to meet you, Isabella," the old woman said.

"How do you know my name?" Isabella asked.

"Because you are a friend of the winds…and so am I," the old woman slowly replied. Then she reached up and gently touched Isabella's beanie.

Pop came out holding two bubblegum-flavored ice cream cones with sprinkles. "This is our treat—it'll be our little secret," he told Isabella. "Scoot over so I can sit down."

"I don't think there's room," Isabella said. But the spot beside her was empty! She looked up and down Main Street, but there was no sign of the old woman.

"Who are you looking for?" Pop asked. "And what is that on your hat?"

Isabella whipped off her beanie. There, hanging just below the propeller, was a wispy, red feather. "The Wind Lady must have given it to me," she said softly.

"The Wind Lady?" Pop wondered, handing Isabella her ice cream cone. "You know, there's an old story around here about a mysterious lady who lives in a cave near the Blowing Rock. They call her 'Wind Keeper'."

I'll bet that lady was Wind Keeper, Isabella said to herself.
But why did she give me a red feather?

When Isabella, Pop, and Mullaby got home, everyone jumped in
the car for the short trip to the Blowing Rock. LuLu spread out a picnic blanket
while Trip and Ginny ran to the big rock and threw a paper napkin over the edge.

Sure enough, a light wind blew it right back up to them.

"See?" Ginny said. "It *is* magic!"

Isabella was now even more convinced that the legend of the Blowing Rock was true. *I have to find out where those winds are coming from,* she thought. She put Mullaby on her leash and headed down a path below the big rock.

"Be back soon for lunch, Isabella," LuLu called. "And be careful!"

Isabella stopped along the path to pick wildflowers for LuLu. Suddenly, she was startled by a big gust of wind. Mullaby yipped loudly, jerked the leash from Isabella's hand, and bolted into the woods.

"Mullaby, come back!" Isabella cried. But as she ran after the frightened dog, another strong wind pushed her through an opening in the rhododendron bushes.

Isabella found herself in a large, breezy cave. Standing before her was the old woman in the colorful shawl. And perched beside her was a large, red tail hawk. "I'm pleased to see you again, Isabella," the old woman said. "I am Wind Keeper. Welcome to the Cave of the Winds. Red Tail and I have been expecting you."

"Expecting me?" Isabella whispered.

Wind Keeper smiled. "You have much to learn, my child," she said kindly. "But, for now, I will teach you the magic powers of the little red feather on your beanie."

Magic powers? Isabella thought. *Wait till Trip hears about this!*

"The feather is Red Tail's," Wind Keeper explained. "It has a special magic to help you fly."

"Fly? Me, fly?" Isabella cried. She had always dreamed of gliding on the winds.

"Listen carefully, Isabella," Wind Keeper said. "When you touch the red feather, the winds will lift you off the ground. Touch it again, and you will return to the ground. But you must use this power only for good. The feather is a gift, so you may help others."

And with that, the old woman disappeared again.

Red Tail flew to a rock ledge next to Isabella and spread his enormous wings. *"Don't be afraid,"* he seemed to say.

Isabella's mind whirred. *Was her feather really magic? Would she be brave enough to fly?*

Suddenly, Isabella heard her dog barking desperately. Mullaby was in trouble!

Isabella dashed out of the cave and up the path, following Mullaby's barks. Finally, she stopped and peered down into a deep ravine. To her horror, she saw that the dog's leash was tangled in a thorn bush. Mullaby was trapped!

"Hold on!" Isabella yelled. "I'll save you!" But the ravine was too narrow and steep for her to reach Mullaby.

Then Isabella remembered her beanie. She took a deep breath, reached up, and touched the red feather with shaky fingers. Almost immediately, the winds around her began to blow. Isabella's body lifted slowly off the ground, just as Wind Keeper had promised!

She couldn't help feeling a tiny bit scared. But Isabella was determined to have courage. She had to help Mullaby.

Suddenly, a bright flash of red appeared in the sky. It was Red Tail! The great hawk swooped close to Isabella and began flying beside her. Isabella felt much safer with the hawk as her companion. Together, they headed toward the ravine.

As she glided over the ravine, Isabella spied a clearing near Mullaby. She touched the feather once again, and floated gently to the ground.

But Isabella froze as soon as she set down. A big, copper-colored snake was right between her and Mullaby— a snake coiled and ready to strike! Isabella stood very, very still as Pop had taught her.

Suddenly, with an ear-piercing screech, Red Tail dove in front of her, his talons bared. In a flash, the hawk snatched the snake off the ground and swooped away.

"Whew," Isabella sighed. "That was close."

Isabella ran to Mullaby and carefully untangled the leash. Mullaby jumped up and covered Isabella's face with big, wet kisses.

And from somewhere in the winds, Isabella heard the voice of Wind Keeper: *"Because of your courage and concern, Isabella, Mullaby is safe. My child, you have done well."*

"Why, Isabella, what beautiful flowers!" LuLu said, admiring the pinkish blossoms.

Trip and Ginny came running up. "Where have you been, Isabella?" Ginny asked.

"Yeah, did you do something fun without us?" said Trip.

Isabella smiled mysteriously. For now, she was going to keep her flying adventure a secret.

That night, Isabella lay in bed gazing out her window at the darkening sky. She could see Red Tail circling lazily above her cottage, keeping watch.

And as her eyes began to close, she again heard Wind Keeper's voice murmuring in the winds: *"Good night, Isabella. Sleep well...for you and Red Tail will have many more adventures."*

Published by Parkway Publishers, Inc.
421 Fairfield Lane
Blowing Rock, NC 28605

Book design by Aaron Burleson

Library of Congress Cataloging-in-Publication Data

Graves, Jonathan, 1943-
Isabella Propeller and the magic beanie / by Jonathan Graves ; illustrated by Gail Haley.
p. cm.
Summary: After an encounter with Wind Keeper, a mysterious mountain woman, Isabella
discovers that her new beanie with a red feather has magical powers.
ISBN 978-1-933251-74-5
[1. Flight--Fiction. 2. Hats--Fiction. 3. Feathers--Fiction. 4. Magic--Fiction.] I. Haley, Gail E., ill.
II. Title.
PZ7.G775236Is 2011
[Fic]--dc23
2011017471

Thanks to Skoshi the Red Tailed Hawk at Charlotte Raptor Center

For more information on Isabella's Blowing Rock, visit:
www.IsabellaPropeller.com
www.BlowingRock.com
www.TheBlowingRock.com

Printed in China

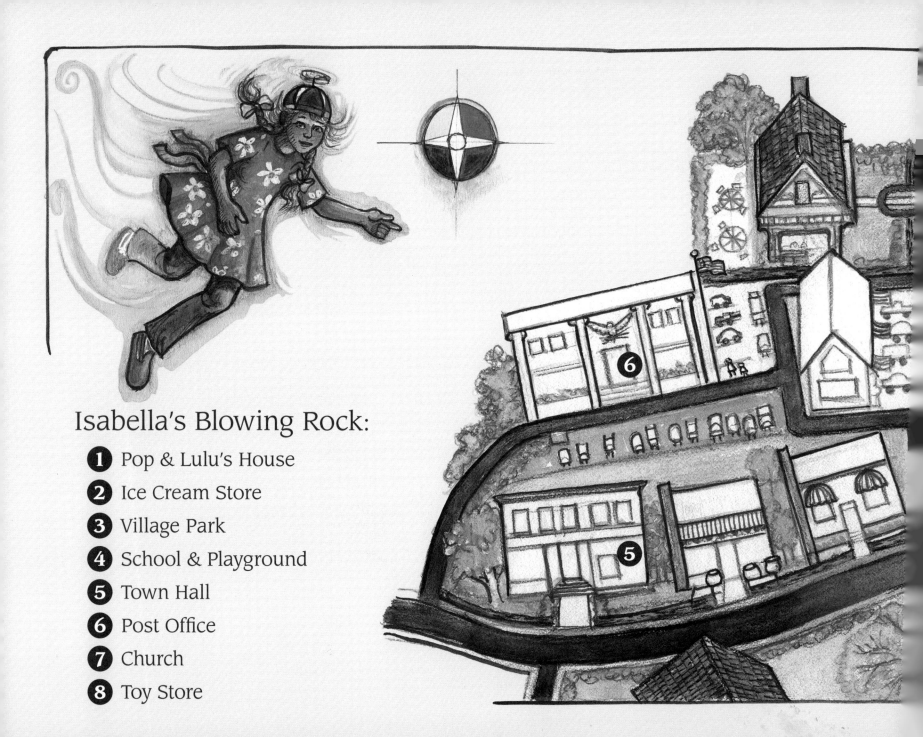

Isabella's Blowing Rock:

1 Pop & Lulu's House
2 Ice Cream Store
3 Village Park
4 School & Playground
5 Town Hall
6 Post Office
7 Church
8 Toy Store